ROBERT E. LEE
(1807–1870)

QUOTATIONS

OF

Robert E. Lee

APPLEWOOD BOOKS
Carlisle, Massachusetts

978-1-55709-055-3

10 9 8 7 6 5 4 3 2 1

MANUFACTURED IN THE UNITED STATES OF AMERICA
WITH AMERICAN-MADE MATERIALS

Robert E. Lee

ROBERT EDWARD LEE, United States and
Confederate soldier renowned as commanding
general for the Confederate States army during
the Civil War, was born January 19, 1807,
at Stratford Hall in Westmoreland County,
Virginia. He was the fifth of six children born
to Revolutionary War officer Henry "Light Horse
Harry" Lee III and his second wife, Anne Hill
Carter. After his father's financial setbacks and
death when Robert was eleven, he was reared
by his mother in northern Virginia. Robert was
accepted to the U.S. Military Academy at
West Point in 1824. Lee graduated second in
his class in 1829.

Robert Lee married Mary Anna Randolph
Custis, great-granddaughter of Martha Custis
Washington, President Washington's wife, in
June 1831. The couple had seven children, three
boys and four girls. When the Mexican-American
War began in 1846, Lee was ordered to oversee
road construction in Mexico but demonstrated
his military prowess in reconnaissance as a
cavalryman. In 1852, Brevet Colonel Lee was
appointed superintendent of the U.S. Military
Academy, serving there for three years.

With the death of his father-in-law in 1857,
wife Mary Custis Lee inherited the family
home, Arlington House, across the river from
Washington, D.C. Failing to find a caretaker for

the plantation, Robert took a two-year leave of duty to run Arlington House. In 1859 as army colonel, Lee put down an abolitionist uprising in Harpers Ferry, and also quelled Mexican incursions in Texas in 1860 before being drawn into the Civil War. While privately Lee opposed the Confederacy, he could not raise arms against his native Virginia. He resigned from the U.S. Army April 20, 1861, and joined the Virginia forces three days later. In June 1862 he was made commander of the Army of Northern Virginia.

Lee's battles produced surprising victories, inconclusive stalemates, and crushing defeats, the largest Confederate casualties occurring at the Battle of Gettysburg in June 1863. By January 1865 Robert E. Lee was promoted to general-in-chief of the Confederate forces. Yielding to disease, desertion, and being decidedly outnumbered, General Lee surrendered to General Grant at Appomattox Court House April 9, 1865. In October 1865 he accepted the post of president of Washington College (today's Washington and Lee University) in Lexington, Virginia, which he held until his death. In the postwar period Lee applied for amnesty, swearing allegiance to the United States, but his application was lost. His citizenship was posthumously restored by a joint resolution of Congress in 1975. Robert E. Lee suffered a stroke in September 1870 and died of pneumonia October 13, 1870. He is buried beneath Lee Chapel at Washington and Lee University.

QUOTATIONS

OF

Robert E. Lee

I hereby accept the appointment to the station of a Cadet in the service of the United States, with which I have been honnoured [sic] by the President.

– Letter to Secretary of War John C. Calhoun, April 1, 1824

*T*he truth is, that I have been for so many years in the habit of repressing my feelings, that I can now scarcely realize that I may give vent to them, and act according to their dictates, but this is fast recurring to me, so you may be prepared for their expression.

– Letter to Mary Anna Randolph Custis, Baltimore, October 30, 1830

*T*he manner in which the Army is considered and treated by the Country and those whose business it is to nourish and take care of it, is enough to disgust every one with the Service, and has the effect of driving every good soldier from it, and rendering those who remain, discontented, careless and negligent.

– Letter to Lieutenant John Mackay, June 27, 1838

*T*o be alone in a crowd is very solitary. In the woods I feel sympathy with the trees and birds, in whose company I take delight, had no experience no pleasure in a strange crowd.

– Letter to wife, Mary Custis Lee, June 4, 1839

R E Lee

I have seen no one here yet that I desire even to behold again.

– Letter to wife, Mary Custis Lee, April 18, 1841

R E Lee

*I*n the event of war with any foreign government I should desire to be brought into active service in the field with as high a rank in the regular army as I could obtain, & if that could not be accomplished without leaving the corps of Engineers, I should then desire a transfer to some other branch of the Service, & would prefer the Artillery. I would however accept no situation under the rank of field officer.

– Letter to chief engineer Colonel Joseph G. Totten, June 17, 1845

I would never advise any young man to enter the Army. He is cut off from all hope of preferment. He performs all the tedium & drudgery of the Service, & no matter how well he may have performed his duties & prepared himself for the Service, as Soon as the opportunity occurs for which he has been preparing, waiting & laboring, a Sett of worthless, ignorant, political aspirants or roués, are put over his head, who in spite of themselves, he has to lug on his Shoulders to victory.

– Letter to brother, Sydney Smith Lee, March 4, 1848

*M*an's nature is so selfish so weak. Every feeling, every passion urging him to Jolly, excess & sin that I am sometimes disgusted with myself & sometimes with all the world.

– Letter to wife, Mary Custis Lee, July 8, 1849

*D*o not dream. It is too ideal, too imaginary. Dreaming by day, I mean. Live in the world you inhabit. Look upon things as they are. Take them as you find them. Make the best of them. Turn them to your advantage.

– Letter to son, Custis Lee, March 1852

*Y*ou must study to be frank with the world, frankness is the child of honest courage.
– Letter to son, Custis Lee, April 5, 1852

R E Lee

*N*ever do a wrong thing to make a friend or keep one. The man who requires you to do so is dearly purchased at a sacrifice.
– Letter to son, Custis Lee, April 5, 1852

R E Lee

*T*here is no more dangerous experiment than that of undertaking to be one thing before a man's face and another behind his back. We should live and act and say nothing to injure of any one. It is not only best as a matter of principle but it is the path to peace and honor.
– Letter to son, Custis Lee, April 5, 1852

R E Lee

*D*uty, then is the sublimest word in our language. Do your duty in all things, like the old puritan. You cannot do more, you should never wish to do less.
– Letter to son, Custis Lee, April 5, 1852

*T*he Abolitionst...must see that he has neither the right or power of operating except by moral means and suasion.

– Speech before the U.S. Senate, March 3, 1854

R.E.Lee

I like the wilderness, and the vicissitudes of camp life, are no hardship to me. I grieve over my separation from my wife & children & the supervision of their interests.

– Letter to Elizabeth Stiles, May 24, 1856

R.E.Lee

*I*f by endeavoring to direct you to virtue & deter you from vice, to shew you the beauty of wisdom & the evil of folly; to inspire you with a love of the noble characteristics of man, & a detestation for the passions of a brute; is deserving of having my "opinions & love less valued," then I am rightly served.

– Letter to son, William Fitzhugh Lee, November 1, 1856

*I*n this enlightened age, there are few I believe,
but what will acknowledge, that slavery as
an institution, is a moral & political evil in
any Country. It is useless to expatiate on its
disadvantages. I think it however a greater evil to
the white man than to the black race, & while my
feelings are strongly enlisted in behalf of the latter,
my sympathies are more strong for the former.
– Letter to wife, Mary Custis Lee, December 27, 1856

REdee

*M*y own troubles, anxieties & sorrows sink
into insignificance when I contemplate the
sufferings present & prospective of the nation.
– Letter to cousin, Martha Custis Williams Carter, January 22, 1861

REdee

*A*s far as I can judge from the papers we are
between a State of anarchy & Civil war....It has
been evident for years that the country was doomed
to run the full length of democracy. To what a
fearful pass it has brought us. I fear mankind for
years will not be sufficiently christianized to bear
the absence of restraint & force.
– Letter to wife, Mary Custis Lee, January 23, 1861

$\mathcal{T}$he South, in my opinion, has been aggrieved by the acts of the North…I feel the aggression, and am willing to take every proper step for redress.
– Letter, January 23, 1861

R E Lee

$\mathcal{S}$ecession is nothing but revolution.
– Letter to son, William Fitzhugh Lee, January 29, 1861

R E Lee

$\mathcal{I}$ look upon secession as anarchy. If I owned the four millions of slaves in the South, I would sacrifice them all to the Union; but how can I draw my sword upon Virginia, my native State?
– Reply to Francis Preston Blair regarding Lincoln's desire to have Lee command the Union army, April 18, 1861

R E Lee

$\mathcal{I}$ have been unable to make up my mind to raise my hand against my native state, my relations, my children & my home. I have therefore resigned my commission in the Army & never desire again to draw my sword save in defence of my State.
– Letter to cousin, John Rogers, April 20, 1861

$\mathcal{D}$eeply impressed with the solemnity of
the occasion on which I appear before you and
profoundly grateful for the honor conferred
upon me, I accept the position your partiality
has assigned me, though I would greatly have
preferred your choice should have fallen on one
more capable.

– Speech before the Virginia Convention on being offered command
of military forces, April 23, 1861

R E Lee

$\mathcal{V}$irginia has to day I understand joined the
Confederate States. Her policy will doubtless
therefore be shaped by united Counsels. I
Cannot Say what it will be. But trust that a
merciful Providence will not turn his face
entirely from us & dash us from the height to
which his Smiles had raised us.

– Letter to cousin, Cassius Lee, April 25, 1861

R E Lee

$\mathcal{W}$hen I reflect upon the calamity impending
over the Country my own sorrows sink into
insignificance.

– Letter to wife, Mary Custis Lee, May 8, 1861

*D*o not grieve for the brave dead. Sorrow for those they left behind friends, relatives & families. The former are at rest. The latter must Suffer.

– Letter to wife, Mary Custis Lee, July 27, 1861

R E Lee

I enjoyed the Mountains as I rode along. The views were magnificent. The valleys so beautiful, The Scenery so peaceful. What a glorious world Almighty God has given us. How thankless & ungrateful we are, & how we labour to mar His gifts. May he have mercy on us!

– Letter to wife, Mary Custis Lee, August 4, 1861

R E Lee

*F*or mil: news I must refer you to the papers. You will see there more than ever occur, & what does occur, the relation must be taken with much allowance. Do not believe anything you see about me.

– Letter to wife, Mary Custis Lee, September 9, 1861

I really believe I am getting to be a young man
but ca'nt realize it; for I feel just as I did ten years
ago; but there is no mistake about it, for I am five
feet ten strikingly handsome, with a strong
tenderly to a mustache & whiskers.

– Letter to sister, Anne Carter Lee, December 1, 1861

R E Lee

*T*he best troops are ineffective without
good officers.

– Letter to Andrew Gordon McGrath, judge of Confederate States
    court, December 24, 1861

R E Lee

I fear our soldiers have not realized the necessity
for the endurance and labor they are called upon
to undergo, and that it is better to sacrifice
themselves than our cause.

– Letter to wife, Mary Custis Lee, February 23, 1862

There is nothing so military as labour, &
nothing so important to an army as to save
the lives of its soldiers.
– Letter to Confederate president Jefferson Davis, June 5, 1862

R E Lee

Still we cannot afford to be idle, and though
weaker than our opponents in men and military
equipments, must endeavor to harass, if we
cannot destroy them.
– Said to Confederate president Jefferson Davis, September 3, 1862

R E Lee

But as those dear to me are diminished, I cling
more anxiously to those who remain.
– Letter to daughter, Mildred Childe Lee, November 3, 1862

R E Lee

It is well that war is so terrible, otherwise we
should grow too fond of it.
– To Colonel James Longstreet regarding the Union army being
   repelled at the Battle of Fredericksburg, December 13, 1862

$\mathcal{Y}$ou must study hard, gain knowledge, and learn your duty to God and your neighbor: that is the great object of life.

– Letter to daughter, Mildred Childe Lee, December 25, 1862

R E Lee

$\mathcal{O}$ld age & sorrow is wearing me away, & constant anxiety & labour, day & night, leaves me but little repose.

– Letter to wife, Mary Custis Lee, March 9, 1863

R E Lee

$\mathcal{T}$here never were such men—in any army before, & there never can be better in any army again. If properly led they will go anywhere & never falter at the work before them.

– Letter to William C. Rives, May 21, 1863

*G*od takes care of us all & calls to him those
he prefers.
– Letter to wife, Mary Custis Lee, June 11, 1863

R E Lee

I shall therefore have to accept battle if the
enemy offers it, whether I wish to or not, and as
the result is in the hands of the Sovereign Ruler
of the universe and known to him only, I deem it
prudent to make every arrangement in our power
to meet any emergency that may arrive.
– Letter to Confederate president Jefferson Davis, July 8, 1863

R E Lee

*H*ow great is my remorse at having thrown
away my time & abused the opportunities
afforded me. Now I am unable to benefit either
myself or others & am recg in this world the
punishment due to my sins & follies.
– Letter to wife, Mary Custis Lee, July 26, 1863

I know how prone we are to censure and how ready to blame others for the non-fulfillment of our expectations. This is unbecoming in a generous people, and I grieve to see its expression.
– Letter to Confederate president Jefferson Davis, August 8, 1863

R E Lee

*T*he general remedy for the want of success in a military commander is his removal…. No one is more aware than myself of my inability for the duties of my position. I cannot even accomplish what I myself desire…I, therefore, in all sincerity, request your Excellency to take measure to supply my place.
– Letter to Confederate president Jefferson Davis, August 8, 1863

R E Lee

*Y*ou say rightly, the more you learn the more you are conscious of your ignorance. Because the more you know, the more you find there is to know in this grand & beautiful world. It is only the ignorant who suppose themselves omniscient. You will find all the days of your life that there is much to learn & much to do.
– Letter to wife, Mary Custis Lee, September 10,1863

We must make up our minds to bear it all,
until a Just & Merciful God avenges us.
– Letter to wife, Mary Custis Lee, April 3, 1864

R E dee

Our life in this world is of no value except
to prepare us for a better. That should be our
Constant aim & the end of all our efforts.
– Letter to wife, Mary Custis Lee, April 23, 1864

R E dee

I think therefore we must decide whether
slavery shall be extinguished by our enemies
and the slaves used against us, or to use them
ourselves at the risk of the effects which may
be produced upon our social institutions.
– Letter to district attorney Andrew Hunter, January 11, 1865

R E dee

I think those who are employed should be freed.
It would be neither just nor wise, in my opinion,
to require them to serve as slaves.
– Letter to Mississippi representative Ethelbert Barksdale,
   February 18, 1865

*B*ut feeling that valor and devotion could accomplish nothing that would compensate for the loss that must have attended the continuance of the contest I determined to avoid the useless sacrifice of those whose past services have endeared them to their countrymen....With an unceasing admiration of your con-staincy and devotion to your country and a grateful remembrance of your Kind and generous consideration for myself, I bid you all an affectionate farewell.
– General Orders No. 9, April 10, 1865

R E Lee

*I*t is with pain that I announce to Your Excellency the surrender of the Army of Northern Virginia.
– Letter to Jefferson Davis near Appomattox Court House, April 12, 1865

A partisan war may be continued and hostilities protracted, causing individual suffering and the devastation of the country, but I see no prospect by that means of achieving a separate independence.

– Letter to Jefferson Davis, April 20, 1865

R.E.Lee

*B*eing excluded from the provisions of amnesty and pardon contained in the proclamation of the 29th ult., I hereby apply for the benefits, and full restoration of all rights and privileges, extended to those included in its terms.

– Letter to President Andrew Johnson, June 13, 1865

R.E.Lee

I am desirous that the bravery of the Army of N. Va shall be correctly transmitted to posterity. This is the only tribute that can be paid to the worth of its noble officers & soldiers.

– Letter to Colonel Walter Taylor, July 31, 1865

I have thought it probable that any occupation of the position of President, might draw upon the College a feeling of hostility; & I should therefore cause injury to an Institution, which it would be my highest desire to advance.

– Letter to trustees of Washington College, August 24, 1865

R.E.Lee

*A*ll should unite in honest efforts to obliterate the effects of war, and to restore the blessings of peace.

– Letter to John Letcher, August 28, 1865

R.E.Lee

I look forward to better days, & trust that time & experience the great teachers of men, under the guidance of an ever-merciful God, may save us from destruction, & restore us the high hopes & prospects of the past.

– Letter to Matthew Fontaine Maury, September 8, 1865

I, Robert E. Lee of Lexington, Virginia do
solemn, in the presence of Almighty God, that
I will henceforth faithfully support, protect and
defend the Constitution of the United States,
the Union of the States thereafter, and that I
will, in like manner, abide by and faithful support
all laws and proclamations which have been
made during the existing rebellion with reference
to the emancipation of slaves, so help me God.
– Amnesty oath to the United States, October 2, 1865

R E Lee

*T*rue patriotism sometimes requires of men to
act exactly contrary, at one period, to that which
it does at another, and that the motive which
impels them—the desire to do right—is precisely
the same.
– Letter to P. G. T. Beauregard, October 3, 1865

Waiting for the action of President Johnson upon my application to him, to be embraced in his proclamation of Amnesty. Believing until that was done, no restoration of rights would be accorded me; & the fact of such an application would merely serve to excite the Radicals, with whom I do not appear to be in favour, to oppose & make more difficult the attainment of the favourable action of the President.

– Letter to brother, Sydney Smith Lee, January 4, 1866

R E Lee

I have thought, from the time of the cessation of hostilities, that silence and patience on the part of the South was the true course; and I think so still.

– Letter to Mrs. Jefferson Davis, February 23, 1866

R E Lee

It will be difficult to get the world to understand the odds against which we fought, and the destruction or loss of all returns of the army embarrass me very much.

– Letter to Jubal A. Early, March 15, 1866

*A*s regards the erection of such a monument as is contemplated; my conviction is, that however grateful it would be to the feelings of the South, the attempt in the present condition of the Country, would have the effect of retarding, instead of accelerating its accomplishment; & of continuing, if not adding to, the difficulties under which the Southern people labour.

– Letter to former Confederate general Thomas L. Rosser, December 13, 1866

R E Lee

I can only say that while I have considered the preservation of the constitutional power of the General Government to be the foundation of our peace and safety at home and abroad, I yet believe that the maintenance of the rights and authority reserved to the States and to the people, not only essential to the adjustment and balance of the general system, but the safeguard of the continuance of a free government.

– Letter to Sir John Acton, December 15, 1866

I hope you will also find time to read and improve your mind. Read history, works of truth, not novels and romances. Get correct views of life, and learn to see the world in its true light.
– Letter to daughter, Mildred Childe Lee, December 21, 1866

R E Lee

*T*he Conservatives are too weak to resist successfully the radicals, who have every thing their own way, & I fear will destroy the Country. I trust that the good sense of the people will yet save it. The tendency seems to be to one vast Government, sure to become aggressive abroad & despotic at home; & I fear will follow that road, which history tell us, all such Republics have trod, Might is believed to be right, & the popular Clamor, the voice of God.
– Letter to nephew, Edward Lee Childe, January 5, 1867

R E Lee

*D*iligence & integrity in any useful pursuit of life will be sure to secure prosperity & fame; and success will result from engaging in that business in which the generosity of mankind are interested.
– Letter to Professor J. B. Minor, University of Virginia, January 17, 1867

The certain fact seems to be that though the war has ended, peace is not restored to the Country.

– Letter to nephew, Edward Lee Childe, January 22, 1867

R E Lee

But when I saw the cheerfulness with which the people were working to restore their condition, and witnessed the comforts with which they were surrounded, a load of sorrow which had been pressing upon me for years was lifted from my heart.

– Letter to son, Fitzhugh Lee, passing through Petersburg, Virginia, December 21, 1867

R E Lee

My only pleasure is in my solitary evening rides, which give me abundant opportunity for quiet thought.

– Letter to daughter, Mildred Childe Lee, March 10, 1868

*T*his day formerly brought great rejoicing to the country, and Americans took delight in the celebration. It is still to me one of thankfulness & grateful recollections, & I hope that it will always be reverenced & respected by virtuous patriots. The memories & principles of the men of the earlier days of the Republic should be cherished & remembered, if we wish to transmit to our posterity the Government in its purity, they handed down to us.

– Letter to cousin, Martha Custis Williams Carter regarding George Washington's birthday, February 22, 1869

R. E. Lee

*T*he reputation of individuals is of minor importance to the opinion which posterity may form of the motives which governed the South in their late struggle for the maintenance of the principles of the Constitution.

– Letter to nephew, Cassius F. Lee, June 6, 1870

R. E. Lee

*M*ay God help the suffering & avert misery from the poor—Good bye.

– Letter to cousin, Martha Custis Williams Carter, August 27, 1870

*I*n fact, when a man desires to do a thing, or when a thing gives a man pleasure, he requires but small provocation to induce him to do it.

– Last letter written to Baltimore lawyer Samuel H. Tagart, September 28, 1870

R.E.Lee

*P*oliticians are more or less so warped by party feeling, by selfishness, or prejudices, that their minds Are not altogether truly balanced. They are the most difficult to cure of all insane people, politics having so much excitement in them.

– Robert E. Lee Headquarters Papers 1850–1876, Virginia Historical Society

R.E.Lee

I cannot consent to place in the control of others one who cannot control himself.

– *Personal Reminiscences, Anecdotes, and Letters of Gen. Robert E. Lee* (1874), by John William Jones

R.E.Lee

*M*adam, don't bring up your sons to detest the United States government. Recollect that we form one country now. Abandon all these local animosities, and make your sons Americans.

– The *Life and Campaigns of General Lee* (1875), by Edward Lee Childe

A true man of honor feels humbled himself when he cannot help humbling others.

– "Definition of a Gentleman" as quoted in *Lee: The American* (1912), by Gamaliel Bradford

R E Lee

O bedience to lawful authority is the foundation of manly character.

– Quoted in *General Robert E. Lee after Appomattox* (1922), by Franklin Lafayette Riley

R E Lee

T each him he must deny himself.

– To a mother asking that her son be blessed, *R. E. Lee: A Biography*, Vol. 4 (1935), by Douglas Southall Freeman

R E Lee

T he education of a man is never completed until he dies.

– Quoted in *Peter's Quotations: Ideas for Our Time* (1977), by Laurence J. Peter